My Weirder School #8

Dr. Nicholas Is Ridiculous!

Dan Gutman
Pictures by
Jim Paillot

HARPER

An Imprint of HarperCollins Publishers

To Eric and Michael Terranova

My Weirder School #8: Dr. Nicholas Is Ridiculous!

Text copyright © 2013 by Dan Gutman

Illustrations copyright © 2013 by Jim Paillot

All rights reserved. Printed in the United States of America.

www.harpercollinschildrens.com

ISBN 978-0-06-204219-4 (lib. bdg.)—ISBN 978-0-06-204218-7 (pbk.)

Typography by Kate Engbring

13 14 15 16 17 CG/RRDC 10 9 8 7 6 5 4 3 2 1

❖

First Edition

Contents

The Big Test

My name is A.J. and I hate tests.

Tests are no fun at all. If you ask me, we should take all the tests and throw them into a giant garbage can.

No, I take that back. If you ask me, we should throw all the tests into a giant *paper shredder.* Shredding paper is cool.

Sometimes my dad lets me shred papers for him at home. I wish I could shred stuff all day long.

Especially tests.

At school the other day, we were minding our own business when our teacher, Mr. Granite, said the most horrible thing in the history of the world.

"Clear off your desks. It's time for a test."

"WHAT?!" everybody yelled.

"Noooooooooooooo!" shouted Michael, who never ties his shoes.

"I didn't study for a test!" shouted Ryan, who will eat anything, even stuff that isn't food.

"That's not fair!" shouted Alexia, this

girl who rides a skateboard all the time.

"You didn't tell us we were going to have a test!" shouted Neil, who we call the nude kid even though he wears clothes.

Everybody was freaking out! It was like we just heard the news that a meteor was about to destroy the earth.*

Well, *almost* everybody was freaking out.

"I *love* tests!" said Andrea Young, this annoying girl with curly brown hair.

"Me too!" said her crybaby friend Emily, who agrees with everything Andrea says. "Tests are fun!"

---

*Hey, if that happened, we wouldn't have to take any more tests!

Those two probably study for tests when they could be watching TV or playing video games and having fun. What is their problem?

"Relax!" said Mr. Granite. "Every student in the state is taking this test today. You don't have to study for it. The Board of Education just wants to find out how much you know."

"I'm bored of education," I announced.

Mr. Granite walked around the room and put a sheet of paper on each of our desks—face down.

"Do you all have a number two pencil?" he asked.

We all started giggling because Mr. Granite said "number two." Everybody knows what "number two" means, and it doesn't have anything to do with pencils. They should really use a different number for pencils so kids wouldn't confuse them with the other number two.

"Take your time," Mr. Granite told us. "These are questions every American should be able to answer. In fact, many of these questions are given to people who want to become citizens of our country."

"What if I don't know the answers?" I asked.

"Don't worry, A.J.," said Mr. Granite. "This test will be a piece of cake."

It didn't look like a piece of cake to *me*. It looked like a piece of *paper*. What did cake have to do with taking a test anyway?

Hey, maybe we were going to get cake after we finished taking the test!

"When I say Go, turn over your test sheet," said Mr. Granite. "Ready . . . set . . . GO!"

A Piece of Cake

I turned over my test sheet and looked at the questions. There were fourteen of them. The top line said we had to fill in the blanks. I grabbed my pencil.

1. Who was the first president?

Well, that was easy. I wrote down the answer—*Abraham Lincoln*. Next!

2. What is the 4th of July?

Any dumbhead knows that. I figured it had to be a trick question, like "What color is the White House?" I wrote down the answer—*It's the 4th day in July.*

Hey, this test wasn't going to be so hard after all.

3. Where was the Declaration of Independence signed?

Hmmm. I had to think about that one for a minute. I've seen my mom and dad sign contracts and stuff at home. I wrote—*At the bottom.*

4. Can you name the thirteen original colonies?

That was simple. I wrote—*Yes, I can.*

5. What are the three branches of our government?

I wasn't sure about this one. Mr. Granite once told us about three somethings, I remembered, so I wrote them down—*The Nina, the Pinta, and the Santa Maria.*

6. Where does freedom of speech come from?

Any dumbhead knows that. I wrote—*Your mouth.*

7. Name one benefit of being a citizen of the United States.

Hmmm, there are lots of good things about our country. But there was only room for one answer, so I wrote—Candy.

8. Who did we fight in the Revolutionary War?

I had no idea who we fought in the Revolutionary War. I looked around to see if I could copy the answer from somebody else. Little Miss Know-It-All was sitting in front of me, and she knows everything.

"*Pssssst!*" I whispered to Andrea. "Who did we fight in the Revolutionary War?"

"I'm not telling," Andrea whispered back. "That would be cheating, Arlo!"

She calls me by my real name because she knows I don't like it. I leaned over to Ryan, who was sitting next to me.

"*Pssssst!* Who did we fight in the Revolutionary War?"

"The Galactic Empire," Ryan whispered to me.

Ryan knows just about everything there is to know about *Star Wars*, so he had to be right. I wrote down—*The Galactic Empire*.

"No talking, please!" said Mr. Granite.

9. Who becomes president of the United

States if the president should die?

Easy! I wrote—*Chuck Norris.*

10. Who makes the laws in the United States?

Again, I wrote—*Chuck Norris.* I was almost finished with the test.

11. Who said, "Give me liberty or give me death"?

I leaned over to Alexia, who was sitting on my other side.

"Pssssst!" I whispered. "Who said, 'Give me liberty or give me death'?"

"Henry," Alexia whispered.

"Henry who?"

"Patrick," Alexia whispered.

"Well, which is it," I asked her. "Henry or Patrick?"

"Both!" she whispered.

"No talking, please!" said Mr. Granite.

I wrote—Henry and Patrick.

12. What are the duties of Congress?

I giggled, because "duties" sounds just

like "doodies," and we're not supposed to talk about that in school. But all I could think about was a bunch of politicians sitting on toilet bowls. I wasn't sure what to write, so I just put down—number two.

13. Who invented the lightbulb?

Hmmm. I had no idea.

"Psssst!" I whispered to Michael, who was sitting behind me. "Who invented the lightbulb?"

"Bob Lightbulb," he whispered back.

Bob Lightbulb? I never heard of anybody named Bob Lightbulb. Michael may have been yanking my chain. But I know that a lot of stuff was named after the people who invented it. Like McDonald's.

And that vacuum cleaner was named after President Hoover. Maybe Michael was right. I wrote—Bob Lightbulb.

14. Who helped the Pilgrims when they came to America?

Hmmm. When the Pilgrims came to America, they probably had to chop down trees, build their own houses, and work on all kinds of do-it-yourself projects like that. So there could only be one answer. I wrote down—Home Depot.

Finally, the dumb test was finished. Andrea was done before anybody else, of course. She was sitting there, all proud of herself. Mr. Granite came around and collected our papers.

"Now, that wasn't so bad, was it?" he asked.

"It was a piece of cake," Andrea announced.

Why is everybody always talking about cake? And why can't a truck full of cakes fall on Andrea's head?*

---

*Hey, where's Dr. Nicholas? I thought this book was supposed to be about Dr. Nicholas. I want my money back!

Bad News

After a few days we all forgot about that dumb test. Life went on. Andrea was annoying, as usual. I had a Pee Wee football game, and my team won. Ryan had his birthday, and his mom brought in brownies for the whole class.

A week later Mr. Granite was trying to

teach us math when an announcement came over the loudspeaker.

"All classes please report to the all-purpose room for an assembly."

"Not again!" yelled Mr. Granite. Every time he tries to teach us math, we get called to an assembly.

We had to walk a million hundred miles to the all-purpose room, which has a dumb name because you can't go scuba diving in there. Neil the nude kid was the line leader. Alexia was the door holder.

When we got to the all-purpose room, I had to sit between Andrea and Emily. Ugh! Andrea's elbow touched my elbow for a second, and I thought I was gonna die.

Our principal, Mr. Klutz, was waiting
for us on the stage. He has no hair at all.
I mean *none*. I bet his head slips off the
pillow when he's trying to sleep at night.

"I just got the results back from the test
you took last week," Mr. Klutz announced.

"I hope we did well," Emily whispered
to Andrea.

"I know *I* got all the answers right,"
Andrea whispered back. "I looked them
up in my encyclopedia when I got home."

"Our school did *horribly*," Mr. Klutz announced.

"WHAT?!" Everybody gasped.

"Ella Mentry School got the *worst* scores in the whole county," said Mr. Klutz, shaking his head sadly. "I went to a meeting, and the principal of Maroa-Forsyth Grade School was laughing at me. Clearly, you children don't know basic history. I hate to say this, but if we don't bring up our test scores, our school is going to be closed."

I jumped up from my seat.

"Yay!" I shouted. "No more school! No more school! No more school!"

I figured *everybody* was going to jump up from their seats and start chanting

"No more school" with me.

I looked around. Nobody else was standing. Nobody else was chanting. Everybody was looking at me.

Oops. I hate when that happens. I sat back down in my seat.

"*You* probably got all the answers

wrong, Arlo!" Andrea whispered to me. "I bet that's why our school did so poorly."

"Your *face* got all the answers wrong," I whispered back at Andrea.

"That doesn't even make any sense, Arlo."

"Your *face* doesn't make any sense," I told Andrea.

Everybody was talking and whispering to each other until Mr. Klutz held up his hand and made a peace sign, which means "shut up."

"I have decided to bring in a professor from the local college to help teach you students history," he announced.

"WHAT!?" Everybody gasped again.

"We don't want to learn history from some boring college teacher," somebody yelled.

Everybody was upset, even some of the teachers.

"Oh, you're going to like Dr. Nicholas," Mr. Klutz told us. "She's a world-famous historian who has traveled everywhere and written many books about history. She was even on *Oprah*."

Everybody gasped and said, "WOW," which is "MOM" upside down.

"What was she doing on Oprah?" asked Ryan.

"She should get off Oprah," said Michael.

"Oprah could get hurt," said Alexia.

"Is Oprah okay?" said Emily.

"Who's Oprah?" I asked.

"Dr. Nicholas will be coming into your classroom to teach you some basic history that everybody should know," said Mr. Klutz. "Then a week from today you'll get a chance to take that test over again. I think that with the help of Dr. Nicholas, you're going to score much higher. And I'll be able to laugh at those other principals. That will be the icing on the cake."

More cake? Why is everybody always talking about cake?

"And now," Mr. Klutz said, with a big sweep of his arm, "I'd like to introduce . . . Dr. Nicholas!"

The Good Old Days

Dr. Nicholas came out on the stage. She looked *really* old. She had white hair tied up in a bun in the back,* and she walked with a cane—really slowly. I've seen *glaciers* move faster than Dr. Nicholas. I could

---

*What's up with that? Buns are for putting your burger on, not for putting on the back of your head.

have run around the block in the time it took her to get to the middle of the stage.

"Wow, that lady is *old*," whispered Ryan.

"She's even older than Mr. Docker," I whispered.

Mr. Docker is our science teacher. I thought *he* was old. But Dr. Nicholas looked old enough to be Mr. Docker's mother!

"She must know a lot about history, because she's about a million hundred years old," whispered Neil the nude kid.

"Yeah, she probably lived through most of it," whispered Alexia.

Mr. Klutz told us to give Dr. Nicholas a round of applause, so we clapped our hands in circles.

"Does anybody have any questions they would like to ask Dr. Nicholas?" said Mr. Klutz.

"Yeah, how old are you?" I asked.

"That's not a nice question to ask a person, A.J.," said Mr. Klutz.

"I don't mind," said Dr. Nicholas. "I'm ninety-two years old and proud of it. How old are *you*, young man?"

"I'm eight years old," I said.

"Eight?" said Dr. Nicholas. "When I was your age, I was nine."

Everybody laughed even though she didn't say anything funny.

"Did you ever meet Abraham Lincoln?" asked Alexia.

"No," said Dr. Nicholas, "but years ago I drove one of his convertibles."

"Were you alive when there were dinosaurs?" asked Michael.

"Oh yes," said Dr. Nicholas. "In fact, I used to ride a dinosaur to school."

I'm pretty sure that Dr. Nicholas was yanking our chain. Everybody knows there were no schools in dinosaur times. Besides, it would be hard to ride a dinosaur. They don't even make saddles for them. Dr. Nicholas would have had to ride the dinosaur bareback.

But maybe she was telling the truth, because old people don't usually make jokes. That's the first rule of being old.

Ryan stood up to ask a question.

"My dad told me that when he was a kid, they didn't have video games or micro-wave ovens or Fruit Roll-Ups," Ryan said. "What was it like when *you* were a kid?"

"Ah, the good old days," said Dr. Nicholas. "When I was your age, we didn't even have *TV*."

WHAT?! Everybody gasped.

No TV? I would *die* without TV. The only good thing about having no TV is that they couldn't have TV Turnoff Week.

The good old days sounded like the *bad* old days to me. If I lived back then, I would have sat around all day saying, "I wish somebody would hurry up and invent TV already, because I'm bored."

"What did you stare at all day?" asked Neil the nude kid. "What did you do for fun?"

"We went out to play," replied Dr. Nicholas.

WHAT?! There was a buzz in the all-purpose room. Everybody was talking to each other.

"You mean, in the out*doors*?" asked Andrea.

"Yes!"

Everybody gasped again.

"Didn't you get sunburned?" asked Andrea.

32

"Didn't your clothes get dirty?" asked Emily.

"What about the bugs?" asked Michael.

"Wasn't it dangerous?" asked Alexia.

"Weren't you afraid of getting hit by a car?" asked Neil the nude kid.

"No, she was afraid of getting hit by a *dinosaur*," I told Neil.

"Oh, it was a *wonderful* time," said Dr. Nicholas. "My friends and I used to play hopscotch, marbles, or hide-and-go-seek. My favorite thing to do was jump rope. Did you ever jump rope?"

"Oh yeah," said Ryan. "My sister has an app called Jump Rope Simulator on her iPad. It's awesome."

"Dr. Nicholas, were you on your school

jump rope team?" asked Andrea.

"Oh, we didn't have a team," said Dr. Nicholas. "We just jumped rope for the fun of it, out in the street."

"You played *in the street*?!" we all shouted.

Now I *knew* she was yanking our chain. You would have to be *crazy* to play in the street! I bet she made up all that stuff about riding dinosaurs and Abraham Lincoln's convertible.

"My friends and I would jump rope *any- where*," Dr. Nicholas told us. "In fact, I feel like jumping rope right *now*."

That's when the weirdest thing in the history of the world happened. Dr. Nicholas pulled a rope out of her pocket. Then she swung it over her head and started jumping over it.

Dr. Nicholas is ridiculous!

Our First
History Lesson

After lunch Dr. Nicholas came into our classroom.

"Clear off your desks," said Mr. Granite. "It's time for our first history lesson with Dr. Nicholas."

"Yay!" shouted all the girls.

"Boo!" shouted all the boys.

Ugh, I hate history. History is dumb. Why do we have to learn about stuff that already happened? Who cares about a bunch of dead dudes who died a million hundred years ago?

Mr. Granite said he would be back in a half an hour. He went to the teachers' lounge, which is a secret room near the front office where no kids are allowed. My friend Billy, who lives around the corner, told me the teachers go to the teachers' lounge to relax in a big hot tub while servants in bathing suits feed them grapes.

Dr. Nicholas picked up a marker and wrote HISTORY IS FUN! on the whiteboard.

"Today," she said, "we're going to learn about the history of the toilet bowl."

WHAT?!

"Toilet bowls have a history?" asked Ryan.

"Of course!" said Dr. Nicholas. "*Everything* has a history."

"Toilet bowls are disgusting," said Emily, wrinkling up her nose.

"I thought history was all about wars," said Andrea, "and the great men and women who changed the world."

"History is about *everything* that came before us and made the world what it is today," said Dr. Nicholas. "And that includes toilet bowls. Did you ever hear the story of Tom Crapper?"

Everybody laughed because Dr. Nicholas said the word "crapper." My mom told me that's a bad word that I should never say to anybody.

"Wait a minute!" Neil said, jumping out of his seat. "Are you going to tell us that the guy who invented the toilet bowl was named Crapper?"

"No," said Dr. Nicholas. "Simple toilet bowls have been around for many centuries. The first toilet you could *flush* was invented back in 1596 by a man named John Harrington."

So the toilet bowl was invented by a guy named John. That made sense.

"What did Tom Crapper do then?" asked Michael.

Everybody laughed because Michael said the word "crapper" again. It's impossible to say the word "crapper" without laughing. That's the first rule of being a kid.

"Tom Crapper was born in 1836, in England," Dr. Nicholas told us. "His father was a steamboat captain. When Tom was fourteen, he went to work for a plumber in London. By the time he was twenty-five, he owned his own plumbing shop. Back in those days, people didn't even *talk* about toilets, and only very rich people owned one."

"What did everybody else use?" asked Ryan.

"Often they used a hole in the ground," said Dr. Nicholas.

"Gross!" everybody shouted.

"During the 1880s, Tom Crapper improved on the flushing toilet bowl," said Dr. Nicholas. "He also opened up a shop and sold toilet bowls to the public. For the first time, regular people could go

to the store and buy a toilet bowl. And the rest is indoor plumbing history."*

"WOW," we all said, which is "MOM" upside down.

"Today, of course, we all have toilet bowls in our own homes," said Dr. Nicholas, "and we owe it all to Tom Crapper."

I jumped up from my seat.

"Hooray for Tom Crapper!" I shouted. "Crapper! Crapper! Crapper!"

I figured *everybody* was going to jump up from their seats and start chanting "Crapper!" with me.

I looked around. Nobody else was

_____

*I dare you to stand up right now, wherever you are, and shout, "Hooray for indoor plumbing!"

standing. Nobody else was chanting. Everybody was looking at me.

I hate when that happens. I sat back down in my seat.

"I still say toilet bowls are disgusting," said Emily.

"You know what's even *more* disgusting than toilet bowls?" asked Dr. Nicholas.

"What?" we all asked.

"*No* toilet bowls!" she said. "Imagine how the world would be different if we didn't have toilet bowls."

"We would probably still be using a hole in the ground," said Neil the nude kid.

Dr. Nicholas told us lots more cool stuff about the history of toilet bowls. The girls were grossed out, but the boys all thought it was hilarious. Just about anything to do with toilet bowls is hilarious.

That's when the door opened. Mr. Granite came back in. I couldn't believe a half hour had gone by so fast.

"I guess our history lesson is over," said Dr. Nicholas.

"Yay!" shouted all the girls.

"Boo!" shouted all the boys.

"We want to learn more about the history of toilet bowls!" said Ryan.

"Yeah, toilet bowls are *cool*," said Michael.

"Who invented toilet paper, Dr. Nicholas?" asked Neil the nude kid.

"We can discuss that another time," she said as she left the room.

Mr. Granite told us to open our math books, but I couldn't stop thinking about Tom Crapper and his toilet bowl. That's when I came up with the funniest joke in the history of the world.

Do you know what Tom Crapper used to draw his first toilet bowl?

A number two pencil!

Get it?

No wonder I'm in the gifted and talented program. I should get the No Bell Prize for that one.*

---

*That's a prize they give out to people who don't have bells.

Our Second History Lesson

My name is A.J. and I *love* history.

History is *cool*. I had no idea that you could learn about the history of the toilet bowl and stuff.

The next day, right after we finished pledging the allegiance, Dr. Nicholas came into our classroom again.

"It's time for another history lesson,"

said Mr. Granite.

"Yay!" shouted all the boys.

"Boo!" shouted all the girls.

Mr. Granite went to the teachers' lounge and said he'd be back in a half an hour.

"What are we going to learn about today?" I asked Dr. Nicholas. "The history of the urinal?"

"Can we learn about the history of snot?" asked Michael. "I've always wondered where it came from."

"It comes from your nose, dumbhead," said Neil the nude kid.

"Oh, snap!" said Ryan.

"Will you teach us about the history of farting?" I asked. "I bet that's really interesting."

We also suggested that Dr. Nicholas teach us about the history of burping, maggots, snakes, and barf.

"You boys are gross!" said Andrea. "I don't think I like history anymore."

"Me neither," said Emily, who always agrees with everything Andrea says.

"That's too bad," said Dr. Nicholas, "because today we're going to learn about the history of . . . Barbie!"

WHAT?!

Barbie?! I didn't want to learn about the history of Barbie. Barbie is for girls.

"I love Barbie!" Andrea shouted, all excited.

"Me too!" said Emily. "Barbie has a history?"

"Oh yes!" said Dr. Nicholas. "*Everything* has a history. It all started in a California garage back in the 1940s. . . ." Me and the guys covered our ears and made humming noises so we wouldn't have to hear about the history of Barbie. But it didn't work. I still heard every word.

". . . Back in those days, Ruth and Elliot Handler owned a company called Mattel that made picture frames," said Dr. Nicholas.

"Isn't Mattel a toy company?" asked Alexia.

"It wasn't back then," said Dr. Nicholas. "But they used the extra scraps of wood to make doll furniture. Soon they discovered that they were making more money from the doll furniture than the picture frames. So they switched to making toys."

"That's interesting!" said Andrea.

"Tell us more!" said Emily.

I thought I was gonna die.

"Back then," Dr. Nicholas went on, "most dolls were baby dolls. But Ruth and Elliot Handler went on a trip to Switzerland, and one day they saw an adult doll called Lilli in a store. They brought one home for their daughter. And do you know what their daughter's nickname was?"

"Dumbhead Ugly Face?" I guessed.

"You are *so* immature, Arlo!" said Andrea. "I bet their daughter's nickname was Barbie."

"That's right!" said Dr. Nicholas. "So in

1959, Ruth and Elliot decided to make
the first Barbie doll. It was eleven and a
half inches tall, and it sold for three dol-
lars. It became the most popular doll in

the world. Two years later, they came out with Barbie's boyfriend, Ken, and he was named after their son."

Dr. Nicholas went on and on talking about the history of Barbie. I thought the half an hour would never end. I kept looking at the clock and waiting for Mr. Granite to come back from the teachers' lounge.

"Are Ruth and Elliot Handler still alive?" asked Andrea.

"No," said Dr. Nicholas. "Ruth passed away in 2002, and Elliot died in 2011. But Barbie lives on. Mattel has sold more than a *billion* Barbie dolls, and every three seconds another one is sold."

"History is interesting!" said Little Miss Perfect.

I hate history.

"Oh, I almost forgot," Dr. Nicholas said. "After a few years, Elliot decided that he wanted a toy for boys. So he came up with the idea of real-looking little metal cars. And in 1968, Hot Wheels was born."

WHAT?! The same people who invented Barbie also invented Hot Wheels?!

"Tell us about the history of Hot Wheels!" said Ryan.

"Yeah!" shouted all the boys.

"Well, it all started back in—"

Dr. Nicholas didn't get the chance to finish her sentence, because Mr. Granite came back from the teachers' lounge.

"I'm afraid we're out of time," Dr. Nicholas said. "We'll learn more about history tomorrow."

"Yay!" everybody shouted.

"I'm really glad we're learning all about history," said Andrea. "But we need to prepare for the big test."

"Yeah, if we don't do better on the test next week, the school will be closed," said Alexia.

"Don't worry about that silly test," said Dr. Nicholas. "It will be a piece of cake."

More cake?

Maybe they were going to give us a test with all the questions written in the icing of a cake. At Ryan's birthday party last year, there was a cake with a photo of Ryan's face on it. I got to eat Ryan's eyeball. It was cool.

All that talk about cake was getting me hungry. That was good, because it was time for lunch.

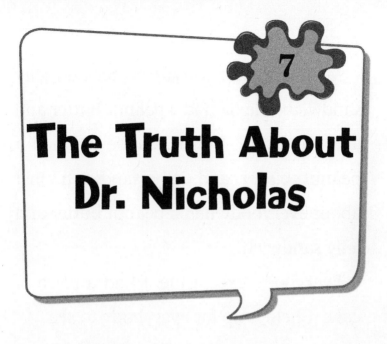

The Truth About
Dr. Nicholas

We have lunch in the vomitorium. It used to be called the cafetorium until some kid threw up in there last year. It was gross.

I sat with the guys and Alexia. Then Andrea and Emily came over, and we had to squeeze together to make room for them.

Michael had a peanut butter and jelly sandwich. Alexia had a peanut butter and jelly sandwich. Neil the nude kid had a peanut butter and jelly sandwich. Just about everybody had a peanut butter and jelly sandwich.

Everybody except me. I had a piece of cake. I held it up for everybody to see.

"Now *this* is a piece of cake!" I told them.

Naturally, we all started talking about Dr. Nicholas and how weird she was.

"If she's a real doctor," I said, "she should cure sick people. That's what doctors do."

"Maybe she cured sick people in history," said Neil.

"She's the weirdest history teacher in

history," Ryan said.

"Yeah," Michael said. "I bet nobody else teaches the history of toilet bowls and Barbie dolls."

"Maybe she's not a real history teacher at all," I said. "Did you ever think about that?"

"What do you mean, A.J.?" asked Alexia.

"Well, maybe Dr. Nicholas kidnapped our real history teacher," I said.

"Old ladies don't kidnap people," Neil said.

"Old ladies don't jump rope either," I told him. "Dr. Nicholas probably kidnapped our real history teacher and sent her back in time with a time machine."

"Stop trying to scare Emily," said Andrea.

"I'm scared!" said Emily.

"Yeah, right now our real history teacher is probably being tortured in a castle during the 13th century. Stuff like that happens all the time, you know."

"We've got to *do* something!" shouted

Emily, and then she went running out of
the vomitorium.

I slapped my head. Sheesh, get a grip!
That girl will fall for anything.

After Emily left, Andrea was sitting there with her worried face on.

"What's the matter with you?" I asked. "Did you lose your encyclopedia?"

"No, I'm worried about our school," Andrea told me. "In just two days, we have to take that test again. Mr. Klutz said the school will close if we don't do better. But we're not going to do very well if we only learn about the history of toilet bowls and Barbie dolls."

I realized Andrea was right for once in her life. Learning about the history of toilet bowls and Barbie dolls was cool, but it wouldn't help us on the test. And if we failed again, Ella Mentry School would be shut down forever. Then we'd have to go to Dirk School, which is a school for dorks on the other side of town.

"What are we going to do?" asked Alexia.

"Beats me," said Neil the nude kid.

Neil looked at me. I looked at Ryan. Ryan looked at Michael. Michael looked at Andrea. Andrea looked at Neil. Everybody was looking at each other.

We were in trouble.

The Study
Buddies

"We should form a study group!"

I couldn't believe those words actually came out of my mouth.

But it made sense. We all knew what was going to be on the test. If we learned the answers together, we'd get them all right, and we could save our school.

"Let's have the study group at *my* house after school this afternoon!" said Andrea. "We can call ourselves the Study Buddies!"

Ugh! One time, I had to put on a jacket and tie and go to Andrea's house for her birthday party. I was so bored that I started throwing snails into the garbage can and hit Emily in the head with one. But I agreed to go over to Andrea's house again to save our school.

"Mom," I said when I got home, "can you drive me over to Andrea's house?"

"What?!" my mother shouted. "You always say you don't like Andrea. Why do you want to go over to her house?"

"We're having a study group."

"WHAT?!" My mom rushed over and put her hand on my forehead. Moms are always putting their hands on your forehead. Nobody knows why. "Are you feeling okay, A.J.? You always say you *hate* studying! Maybe you're coming down with something. You need to rest in bed."

"No!" I told her. "I need to get to Andrea's house right away! It's *very* important!"

My mom drove me over to Andrea's house.

"Hi Arlo!" Andrea said when she opened the door. "You're the first one here. Come on in. Let's go to my room."

My mom went to the kitchen to make chitchat with Andrea's mom. Andrea took me upstairs to her room. It was the weirdest place in the history of the world. There were books and encyclopedias and Barbies and all kinds of pink stuff *everywhere*. I thought I was gonna die.

Luckily, the doorbell rang. It was Ryan and Michael. Andrea and I ran downstairs to let them in.

"*Oooooh!*" Ryan said. "A.J. got to Andrea's

house *first*. They must be in *love!*"

"When are you two Study Buddies gonna get married?" asked Michael.

If those guys weren't my best friends, I would hate them.

Soon the others showed up, and we went to Andrea's basement. And you'll never believe in a million hundred years what was down there.

A classroom!

There was a big whiteboard on the wall, and desks, encyclopedias, posters, and a computer. There was even a flag, so Andrea could pledge the allegiance at home.

Who has a classroom in their basement?

What is Andrea's problem?

We all took seats. Andrea went up to the whiteboard and wrote HISTORY IS FUN! on it.

"I'd like to call this meeting of the Study Buddies to order," she said. "Who can tell me the name of the first president?"

"Wait a minute," I shouted, "you're not a teacher!"

"But I know all the answers for the test, Arlo," Andrea said. "Do *you*?"

"Sure I do," I told her.

"Oh, yeah?" Andrea said. "Who was the first president?"

"Abraham Lincoln," I said. "So nah-nah-nah boo-boo on you."

Everybody laughed even though I didn't say anything funny.

"It was George Washington, dumb-head," Neil whispered to me.

"I knew that," I lied.

Bummer in the summer! I wanted to go to Antarctica and live with the penguins.

We went over all the questions that were on the test, and I found out that I got a few of them wrong the first time. I learned that we fought England in the Revolutionary War. Not the Galactic Empire. I learned that if the president dies, the vice president becomes president. Not Chuck Norris. I learned that Thomas Edison invented the lightbulb. Not Bob Lightbulb.

After a million hundred hours of studying, you'll never believe who poked her head into the basement door.

Nobody! If you poked your head into a door, it would hurt. But you'll never believe who poked her head into the door*way*.

It was Andrea's mom! She looks just like Andrea but with wrinkles. She was with my mom. And they had a big plate full of chocolate chip cookies!

"You kids are working very hard," Andrea's mom told us. "You could be home playing video games and having fun. But here you are learning about history."

"I'm so proud of you!" said my mom.

She was just about to cry, so I was

allowed to eat five cookies. Soon the other parents showed up to take everybody home. We had learned all kinds of history stuff that we didn't know before.

I was ready to kick butt on the big test.*

---

*Grown-ups get mad when you say "butt." Nobody knows why.

The Time Boat

When we got to school the next morning, there was a sign on our classroom door. . . .

GO TO THE SCIENCE ROOM

Hmmm, that was weird.

We went to the science room, which is

all the way at the other end of the school. And you'll never guess in a million hundred guesses what was in the middle of the science room.

Wrong. It was a boat!

WHAT?!

A giant rowboat was in the middle of the room! It was the weirdest thing in the history of the world! Mrs. Yonkers, our computer teacher, was in the science room too, along with Mr. Docker and Dr. Nicholas.

"Where did you get a boat?" I asked.

"From Rent-A-Boat," said Dr. Nicholas. "You can rent anything. But this isn't just *any* old boat. It's a *time* boat."

"What's a time boat?" asked Andrea.

"A time boat is a boat that travels through time," said Mr. Docker. "Mrs. Yonkers and I invented a time machine, with the help of Dr. Nicholas of course."

"Are we going to travel through time?" asked Alexia.

"Yes!" said Dr. Nicholas. "I figured the best way for you children to learn history would be to go there and see it for yourself."

"Yay!" we all shouted.

Traveling through time is the coolest. I saw a movie once about a guy who traveled back in time. When he got there, he killed his mother by accident. So he was never born. That movie was weird.

"Wait a minute," said Michael. "Why do we need a boat? Why didn't you just build a time machine out of a phone booth or a car?"

"Because the whole class can't fit inside a phone booth or a car," said Mrs. Yonkers.

"Hop in!" said Dr. Nicholas.

We all climbed into the time boat. I sat in the front with the guys and Alexia. Andrea and Emily sat in the back.

"Where are we going?" asked Neil the nude kid.

"You will be traveling back to the year 1776," said Dr. Nicholas. She was fiddling with a bunch of knobs on the control

panel of the time boat.

"Are you coming with us?" asked Ryan.

"Oh no," said Dr. Nicholas. "There's no room for grown-ups in the time boat."

"Do we need to paddle or anything?" asked Michael.

"No. Just hold on tight!"

"Aye, aye, Captain!" I said.

It was exciting. The closest I ever came to traveling through time was when my family went to a restaurant called Medieval Times. They had these guys on horses charging at each other with spears while we ate chicken. That place was weird.

"I'm scared!" said Emily, who is scared of everything.

"Don't be afraid," said Dr. Nicholas. "You have nothing to fear but fear itself."

"What does that mean?" I asked.

"Beats me," said Ryan.

"On your mark," yelled all the grown-ups, "get set . . . GO!"

Suddenly, the lights went out. It was so dark, I couldn't see my own hand in front of my face. Then there was a buzzing sound, and the time boat began to rumble and shake. There was electricity in the air.

Well, not really. If there was electricity in the air, we would all die.

"Help!" yelled all the girls. Everybody was freaking out.

We were going back in time! I held on

to the side of the time boat. There were flashing yellow lights and strange noises. It went on for a long time.

And then, suddenly, everything stopped.

A spotlight fell on a lady who was sitting on a chair next to the time boat. She was dressed in old-time clothes, and she was sewing stars onto a flag. She looked a lot like our librarian, Mrs. Roopy.

"Who are you?" asked Andrea.

"I'm Betsy Ross," the lady replied.

"Wow!" I said. "My mom loves your song 'Stop! In The Name Of Love.'"

"That's *Diana* Ross, dumbhead!" said Ryan.

"You look a lot like Mrs. Roopy," said Neil.

"Never heard of her," said the lady who called herself Betsy Ross.

"What are you doing?" asked Emily.

"What does it look like?" Betsy Ross said. "I'm making an American flag."

"Why don't you just go to a store and *buy* a flag?" I asked her.

"They don't sell American flags in stores here in 1776," Betsy Ross told us. "I'm making the first one. You see, we colonists are sick and tired of British rule. So we're starting a revolution."

Betsy Ross told us all about the Revolutionary War. But suddenly, while she was talking, the lights went out. The time boat started shaking and rumbling. There were bright lights flashing. Everybody was freaking out again.

And then the lights went back on. We were back in the science room with Dr. Nicholas and Mrs. Yonkers.

"That was cool!" I said. "We got to see Diana Ross, live and in person!"

"It was almost like a ride at an amusement park," said Neil.

"Do you think we *really* traveled through time?" asked Ryan.

"I don't know," said Michael. "That lady seemed pretty real."

"Can we do it again?" asked Andrea.

"Sure," said Dr. Nicholas as she went over to the control panel. "This time you're going to go back to the year 1920."

Dr. Nicholas fiddled with the knobs. The lights went out, the time boat started shaking, and the next thing we knew, there was a guy standing next to us. He looked a lot like Mr. Docker, and he was holding a bowl of peanuts.

"Who are you?" we asked.

"My name is George Washington Carver," he replied. "I'm an inventor."

"You look a lot like Mr. Docker," I told him. "With a wig."

"Never heard of him," the guy said. "I was born a slave, but I grew up to become one of the most famous scientists in the world. I took peanuts and made them into peanut butter, paper, ink, oils, and over three hundred other products."

"WOW," we all said, which is "MOM" upside down.

George Washington Carver told us all

about peanuts and even let us eat some.
That guy was nutty for peanuts! Then
the lights started flashing again, the time
boat started shaking, and we were back in
the science room.

After that we got to go back in time to meet Susan B. Anthony (who looked a lot like Miss Small, our gym teacher), Thomas Edison (who looked a lot like Mr. Macky, our reading specialist), and Grandma Moses (who looked a lot like Dr. Nicholas). It was the greatest day of my life. You should have *been* there!

"That was cool!" we all said when the lights went back on.

"I'm glad you enjoyed the time boat," Dr. Nicholas told

us. "But you'll have to get out now and let the other classes take their turns."

We were about to climb out of the time boat when the weirdest thing in the history of the world happened.

Somebody screamed!

Well, that's not the weird part, because people scream all the time. The weird part was what happened next.

"Eeeeeeeeeeeeeek!"

It was Andrea.

"What's the matter?" we all asked.

"Emily's not here!" shouted Andrea. "She was sitting right next to me in the time boat!"

"Where's Emily?"

"Where's Emily?"

"Where's Emily?"

In case you were wondering, everybody was shouting, "Where's Emily?"

Emily was gone!

An Emergency

"Emily!"

"Emily!"

"Emily!"

"I'm sure she's around here somewhere," said Dr. Nicholas.

We looked under all the desks in the science room for Emily, but we couldn't find her anywhere.

"Maybe she got scared by all the lights and noise," I said. "She probably ran away. She does that all the time."

"With all that shaking," Ryan said, "she might have fallen out of the time boat."

"They should really put seat belts on time boats," I suggested.

"If Emily fell out of the time boat," said Alexia, "she could be in another time!"

"I think we may have left her back in 1776 with Betsy Ross!" shouted Andrea. "That was the last time I saw her. She'll be stuck in 1776 *forever*!"

Andrea started crying. The grown-ups tried to calm her down, but it was no use. Andrea was freaking out.

"There, there," said Dr. Nicholas as she

patted Andrea on the back.

People always say, "There, there," and pat you on the back when they want you to calm down. They don't say, "There." It has to be "There, there." What's up with that? Why should I feel better just because somebody said the word "there" twice and patted me on the back?

"Emily is my best friend!" Andrea wailed. "Now she's stuck in 1776 for the rest of her life, and I'll never see her again!"

I don't even *like* Emily, but I was getting a little choked up myself.

"She might get shot by British soldiers," said Ryan.

"Or she might help George Washington

cross the Delaware," said Neil the nude kid.

That's when I got a genius idea.

"Hey," I said, "why don't we just get back in the time boat, go to 1776, and look for Emily?"

"Yeah!" everybody shouted.

"That's a great idea, A.J.!" said Dr. Nicholas.

No wonder I'm in the gifted and talented program.

We were climbing back into the time boat when you'll never believe who walked into the science room.

I'm not going to tell you.

Okay, okay, I'll tell you.

It was Emily!

"Emily!" we all screamed.

Everybody ran over to Emily and started hugging her.

"What's the big deal?" Emily said. "Why is everyone shouting and yelling?"

"Where *were* you?" Andrea asked. "We were so worried! We thought that we left

you in 1776, and you would be stuck there for the rest of your life!"

"I wasn't in 1776," Emily explained. "I was in the bathroom."

Oh.

"Why didn't you just wait until we got out of the time boat?" Andrea asked her.

"It was an emergency," Emily whispered. "I had a number two."

"But why did you go to the bathroom?" I asked. "We have plenty of pencils right here."

Emily is weird.*

---

*The underside of a horse's hoof is called a frog. This has nothing to do with the story, but I thought you might like to know.

Good-bye

The next day we had to take the history test again. Everybody was nervous. If we scored high, our school would stay open. But if we scored low, our school would shut down, and we would have to go to Dirk School on the other side of town. We were all on pins and needles.

Well, not really. We were sitting on chairs. Why would anybody want to sit on pins and needles? That would hurt.

Before the test we had to go to the all-purpose room. Mr. Klutz, Mr. Docker, Mrs. Yonkers, and some of the other teachers were up on the stage. But not Dr. Nicholas.

"Where's Dr. Nicholas?" whispered Michael.

"Where's Dr. Nicholas?" whispered Andrea.

"Where's Dr. Nicholas?" whispered Emily.

In case you were wondering, everybody was whispering, "Where's Dr. Nicholas?"

Mr. Klutz made the shut-up peace sign

with his fingers, and we all stopped whispering to each other. He wasn't smiling like he usually is. He looked really sad.

"I wanted to let you students know that I just fired Dr. Nicholas," he said.

WHAT?! Everybody gasped.

We *liked* Dr. Nicholas. This was the worst thing to happen since TV Turnoff Week!

"Why did you fire Dr. Nicholas?" we all shouted.

"I found out she was wasting valuable classroom time to teach you about silly things like the history of Barbie dolls and the history of toilet bowls," said Mr. Klutz. "As a result, you are not prepared for the big test, and you may very well fail it. Ella Mentry School may close its doors forever."

Everybody was moaning, sobbing, and wiping their eyes with tissues.

"I just wanted you to know that it has been a pleasure being your principal," said Mr. Klutz, "and I just wanted to say good-bye."

It was really sad. We walked back to our classroom without saying a word. When Mr. Granite passed out the test papers and asked us if we all had our number two pencils, nobody even giggled or cracked a joke about number two.

"When I say Go, turn over your test

papers," said Mr. Granite. "Ready ... set ... GO!"

I turned over my test paper and looked at the first few questions. . . .

1. Who invented Barbie?

2. What did Tom Crapper do?

Well, you probably know what happened after that. We did *great* on the test. We scored so high that Mr. Klutz threw us a big party. And do you know what I had to eat at the party?

I'm not going to tell you.

Okay, okay, I'll tell you.

NO, IT WASN'T CAKE!

You thought I was going to say a piece of cake, didn't you? But there was no cake at all. Why is everybody always talking about cake?

We had cookies and Jell-O and pie at the party! I ate so much that I thought I was gonna throw up. It was the greatest day of my life.

Maybe Dr. Nicholas will get hired again to teach us more history. Maybe a meteor will destroy the earth, and we won't have to take tests anymore. Maybe they'll come up with a different number for pencils. Maybe the Pilgrims will go to Home Depot. Maybe Chuck Norris will run for

president. Maybe we'll go scuba diving in the all-purpose room. Maybe Dr. Nicholas will get off Oprah. Maybe the dinosaurs will return, and we can ride them to school. Maybe we'll find out who invented toilet paper. Maybe we'll get another ride in the time boat. Maybe we'll get to try some paper made out of peanuts. Maybe Emily will get lost in time for real. Maybe we'll learn how to say the word "crapper" without giggling. Maybe people will stop talking about cake all the time.

But it won't be easy!